LONG AGO
AND FAR AWAY

A collection of short stories

by
George Beale

Illustrations by
Sharon Heaney

Published by
STRANMILLIS COLLEGE
HISTORY DEPARTMENT/LEARNING RESOURCES UNIT

Supported by
DEPARTMENT OF EDUCATION (NI)

This collection of stories is a companion volume to **Long Ago in Ireland**, a collection of stories from Ireland.

ISBN   0   903009 11 0

Contents

Acknowledgements

Designer:
Brian McAleese

Typesetting:
Aoife McEvoy

Design Assistance:
The Northern Ireland Centre for Learning Resources

Editorial Assistance:
Carol Dunbar

STORIES
FROM
SCOTLAND

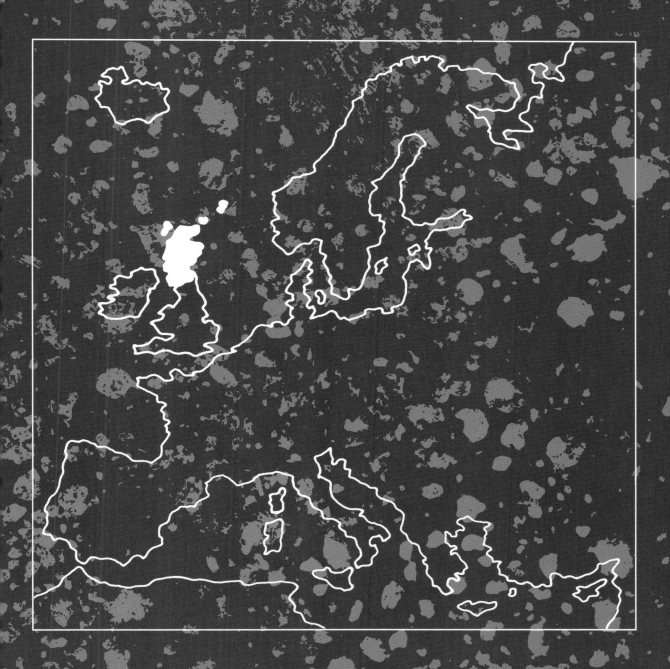

Thomas the Rhymer

Long ago in Scotland, there lived a man called Thomas Learmont. Thomas lived alone in a little thatched cottage in the village of Ercildourne. From the window of his cottage he could see the Eildon Hills where he loved to walk. He watched the animals and birds and studied the trees and flowers. As he walked, he often played the lute and sang, for he enjoyed music very much.

THE EILDON HILLS (© **Scottish Tourist Board/Still Moving**)

Early one summer morning, Thomas left his cottage to visit friends who lived in the hills some distance from his home. It was sunny and hot. After walking for several hours, he felt tired and sat down to rest beside a bubbling stream at the edge of a shady wood. He began to pluck the strings of the lute and play a little tune. Suddenly, above the strains of his music, Thomas could hear the sound of horses' hooves. In the distance, just beyond the wood, he saw a beautiful lady riding a handsome white horse. The horse galloped towards him and stopped beside the little stream. When the lady dismounted before him, Thomas could see just how

beautiful she really was. Her blue eyes sparkled, her golden hair shimmered as it hung loosely to her shoulders. She wore a long, blue, silk dress and a flowing robe of a darker blue. On her head a crown of precious stones glistened in the morning sunshine.

At once, Thomas jumped to his feet. Then he bowed.

"Your Majesty," he whispered, for he was sure that she was a queen.

"Thomas of Ercildourne," said the lady, "I am the Queen of Elfland, and I have come to visit you. The music you have been playing sounds so sweet and soothing. Play some more for me please."

Thomas took his lute and played such tuneful music as he had never played before. When he had finished, the queen was delighted.

"I have enjoyed your music very much," she said. "You have entertained me admirably. Now you may have a wish."

Thomas was entranced by the queen's beauty. Shyly, he approached her, taking both her hands in his.

"Oh Queen, may I kiss you?" he asked nervously.

"If you kiss me, Thomas," replied the queen, still holding his hands, "you will immediately fall into my power and you will have to serve me for seven years."

"Seven years will pass quickly in your presence, Your Majesty," answered Thomas. Then he kissed her.

The queen mounted the white horse. Thomas climbed up behind her. They galloped over moorland and mountain. After several hours they stopped to rest at a place where three roads met. One road was narrow and winding with tall, prickly thorn bushes on each side. The second road was broad and straight with flowers growing along the hedgerows. The third road was the prettiest of them all. It led over heather-clad hills, and yellow bracken could be seen far into the distance.

"Well, Thomas," said the queen, "three roads lie before us. The first road with the thorn bushes appears a difficult and dangerous road. Few people ask where it leads. If more asked, it is likely that they would travel along it, for it is the Path of Righteousness and leads to a glorious city. The second road appears much easier and looks so pleasant, but there are dangers all the way which, at first, the traveller cannot see. Many choose this road, but are often sorry they did, for it is the Path of Wickedness and leads to destruction. Thomas, we shall take the third road - the prettiest of them all - for it leads to Elfland - my home."

"When shall we arrive at your land?" asked Thomas.

"Tonight," replied the queen. "Remember, the moment you enter my country, you must not speak a word. All the time you will be there you must remain silent. Then, after seven years, you will return to your own land. But remember, if you speak even a single word, never again will you see your own home. You will be doomed to wander for ever in the vast wilderness between Elfland and your own country."

Over the heather-clad hills they galloped. Along the road lined with yellow bracken they galloped. Through the darkness they rode, across raging streams and close to the edge of steep cliffs, until at last they reached Elfland.

There, everything was bathed in a most beautiful light. Trumpets sounded as they entered the gates and climbed to the jewelled palace on the hill.

During his stay in Elfland, Thomas saw many wonderful sights, but not a single word did he speak. Then, when he had served the queen for seven years, the time came for him to leave. The queen

herself led him through the beautiful castle garden, down the hill to the gate. As they parted, the queen plucked an apple from a tree and gave it to Thomas.

"Take this apple as a parting gift," she said. "It is a magic apple. From this time you will always speak the truth. And remember this Thomas, one day I shall send two of my servants to bid you return to this land. Until then, farewell."

Thomas, still entranced by the beauty of the queen, suddenly became drowsy. The sights and colours of Elfland faded away and he fell into a deep sleep. When he woke, he found himself beneath a tree in the little wood where he had rested seven years ago. He picked up his lute and wandered in the sunshine back to his cottage. As Thomas passed through the village, an old lady fainted when she saw him for she thought he had been dead for years. However, Thomas assured the villagers that they need have no fear and told of his adventure. Every word Thomas spoke was true. From the time he arrived home he was able to prophesy and tell of future events. He even prophesied in verse and so he became known as Thomas the Rhymer. Many kings and princes heard of his gift of prophecy and summoned him for advice. They rewarded him greatly and soon he became very rich. He built a castle and every year all the villagers were invited to a great feast.

One night, during one of the feasts, fourteen years after Thomas had returned from Elfland, one of the soldiers on guard at the castle gate ran into the banquet hall. Immediately, he rushed towards Thomas who was playing the lute and singing.

"Master, I have seen a most unusual sight. A milk-white hart and a milk-white hind are walking around the castle walls."

"This is rather strange," said Thomas. "Let's go outside and see."

Thomas and the soldier left the castle hall and, followed by the guests, they went outside to view the strange sight.

When Thomas saw the two deer, he realised at once why they had come. Stepping slowly towards them, he patted them. A feeling of happiness and contentment overcame him as, with an animal on either side, he walked into the dark forest, never again to return to the village of Ercildourne.

The Prophecy of the Birds

In the highlands and islands of Scotland, the raven was considered the wisest and cleverest of all the birds. Many people believed that if a child took his first sip from a raven's skull, he would receive very special powers.

Long ago, a chieftain wished to see if there was any truth in this ancient story. He gave his young son Shamus his first drink of milk from the skull of that wise and clever bird.

As the years passed, there was no sign that Shamus was any different from the other boys of his age. He climbed trees, and ran and jumped. He laughed and played in the hills and by the loch. He seemed just like any ordinary boy.

One day, when the chieftain was walking in the garden of his castle, he saw Shamus sitting under an apple tree. The boy was looking up into the boughs of the tree and making strange sounds. As the chieftain approached, there was a sudden flutter of wings and several small birds flew out from the branches.

"Oh father, you have frightened the birds away!" exclaimed Shamus. "They were telling me about their travels - how, before winter, they leave our shores and fly to warm and sunny lands. There the sky is always blue and the sea laps peacefully against the sandy shores."

"The birds are chirping in their own language," said the boy's father.

"They are," replied Shamus, "but I understand what they say and I can speak to them in their own language too."

It was then that the chieftain realised the truth of the story of the raven's skull!

As Shamus grew older he still talked to many of the birds. Some told him of their travels to distant lands. Others spoke of their adventures in the craggy mountains of Scotland. Shamus became a wise and courageous young man and the members of his clan wished him to succeed his father as chieftain when the time would come.

One night, at supper, when Shamus was serving his father with wine, the chieftain looked up to the rafters of the great hall. Birds had rested there for years and every night during supper they chattered and chirped.

"The birds are very noisy tonight, my son," remarked the chieftain. "I wonder what they are chattering about."

"I know, father," replied Shamus rather nervously. "But if I tell you I am afraid you will be very angry."

The chieftain became even more curious and insisted that Shamus should translate the birds' language for him. Eventually, Shamus agreed.

"Father," he hesitated, "the birds foretell that one day in the future, you will serve me in this very hall."

When the chieftain heard this he was furious. He threw down his goblet, jumped to his feet and ordered his son to leave the castle at once - never to return.

"My own son, a traitor! How can you betray me?" cried the father.

Shamus assured his father that he would always be loyal to him, and that he would never betray him. But the chieftain was determined that his son should leave the country.

Sadly, that night Shamus left the castle. He walked for miles and miles until he found a boat ready to sail for France. Shamus was lucky, for the captain of the ship gave him a job as a member of the crew.

The ship sailed for several days, often tossed about on the stormy sea, until it reached the coast of France. There, Shamus left the ship hoping to find happiness in that new land. He wandered through the beautiful countryside until, through the trees, he could see the sturdy, grey walls of a castle. As the boy approached the gate, he could hear the chattering of birds. He looked up and there, to his amazement, he saw hundreds of sparrows flying round and round above his head. Suddenly, one of the king's guards stepped out from behind a tree.

"Where are you going? Why are you here?" asked the guard.

"I have travelled many miles across land and sea," replied Shamus. "I have come to this land to seek my fortune. I would like some shelter for the night."

"I will lead you to the king," said the guard. "Follow me."

Briskly, Shamus followed the guard along the broad path to the castle. On each side of the path woodcutters chopped down tree after tree. Above their heads the birds hovered and soared, chattering ceaselessly.

"The birds are very noisy," remarked Shamus.

"They chatter all day long," said the guard. "They live inside the castle as well and the king is nearly at his wits' end. He doesn't know what to do to get rid of them."

Soon Shamus and the guard reached a large room where the king's advisers were trying to discuss the castle business. The birds were everywhere - some perched on the rafters, others crouched on every ledge or hovered above the heads of the king's counsellors. Then the guard escorted Shamus to a small room which had no windows. There, the king sat in despair. Just as soon as Shamus entered the room, in flew a sparrow chirping merrily as it landed beside the king.

"Who will rid me of this plague of birds?" asked the king.

"Your Majesty," said Shamus, "I may be able to help you, for I understand the language of the birds."

The king smiled.

"If you are speaking the truth and you are able to rid me of these birds, you will receive a great reward," he replied.

"Your Majesty," said Shamus, "there must be some reason why the sparrows chatter ceaselessly in your castle. I shall find out."

Shamus turned to the little sparrow which had flown into the tiny room. He spoke to it in its own language and discovered what the king needed to know. Then he turned to the king and explained the sparrow's story.

"Oh King," said Shamus, "there is a simple solution to your problem. The sparrows are angry because you have ordered the woodcutters to fell the trees where they build their nests. If you order the woodcutters to stop this work, the birds will leave the castle."

Immediately, the king left the little room and ordered the woodcutters to stop their work that very minute. As soon as the last axe had been laid down, the birds gathered in large flocks from every part of the castle. They flew out of the castle windows and began to build their nests in the trees.

The king was overjoyed, and, as he had promised, he rewarded Shamus for his help. He gave him his finest ship, a company of sailors and a large amount of gold.

Shamus sailed far and wide. He visited many lands and gained great wealth. But after many years of travel he often wished to visit his homeland again. One day, he decided to return. As his fine ship sailed into a tiny island harbour, the villagers lined up along the narrow quayside. They escorted Shamus and his crew to the chieftain's castle.

That night, at the castle, a great feast was prepared in their honour. During the meal, according to a local custom, the old chieftain served his guests with wine. As he poured some wine into Shamus's goblet, the young man remarked, "The prophecy of the birds has come true father! Many years ago they foretold that one day in this very hall, you would serve me. Please receive me as your son again."

Tears welled up in the old chieftain's eyes.

"Oh my son, my son!" he cried. "You shall have all I possess. I am so glad you have returned."

When the King of Scotland heard of Shamus's adventures and of how wise and courageous he had been, he gave him some land on a rocky island. There he built a castle to guard the shores and lived happily among the islanders until he died.

EILEAN DONAN - TRADITIONAL SITE OF SHAMUS'S CASTLE (© **Scottish Tourist Board/Still Moving**)

STORIES
FROM
NORWAY

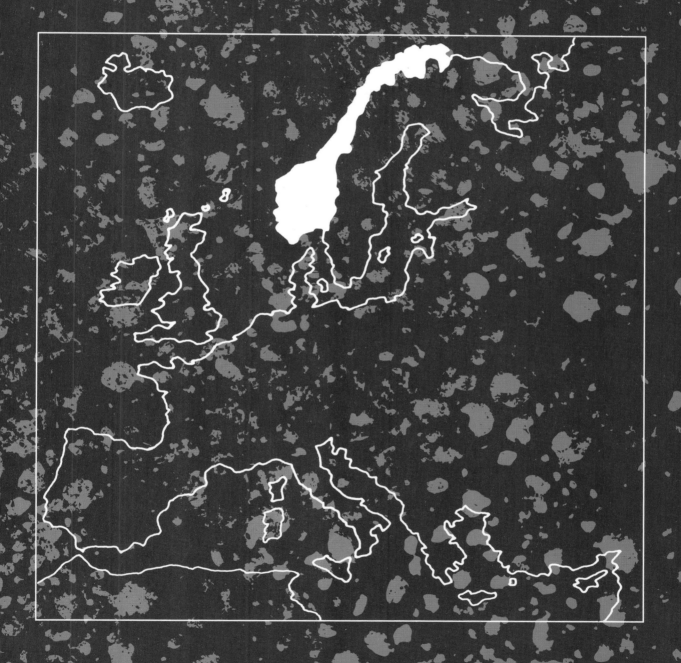

Building the Wall of Asgard

Long ago, when the gods were building Asgard - their kingdom - a builder, who was a giant, appeared and offered his help.

"I can build a wall that will protect your kingdom from all the giants in the world," said the builder, "and the work will be completed in three years."

"What will this work cost?" asked the gods.

"For such a difficult task," replied the builder, "you must give me the sun and the moon, as well as the goddess Freyja for my wife."

The gods, Loki, Odin, and Thor, met together to discuss the builder's terms. They all thought the price was too high. Then Loki, who was a mischief-maker, suggested a plan.

"Let's make a bargain with him," he said. "We'll tell him that if he completes the work in a single winter, he will have what he asked. But if, on the first day of spring, there is even one stone out of place, he will receive no payment."

"He'll never agree to that," answered the gods.

"Well, it's certainly worth a try," said Loki.

When the builder heard the terms of the bargain he was disappointed. Nevertheless, he agreed to accept. The gods allowed him to use his horse Svadilfari to help him and on the first day of winter he began to build.

The builder worked very hard, day after day and night after night. His horse worked even harder. The gods were surprised to see the number of huge rocks this horse could pull.

As the cold winter days passed, the building of the wall progressed steadily. It became higher and stronger each day, until just three days before the end of winter, only part of the city gate remained unfinished.

When the gods saw how much work had been done during the winter months and how little work had to be completed, they were very worried. They met together to discuss what they should do.

"Loki, you are the mischief-maker who suggested this plan, it's up to you to find a way of cheating this builder out of his wages," cried the gods.

"Do not fear," replied Loki, "all will be well."

That evening, when the builder led his horse to collect the last load of stones to complete the gate-posts, a beautiful white mare ran out of the woods and whinnied. Svadilfari looked up and when he saw

the mare trotting through the woods, he broke his harness and galloped after her, leaving the builder alone.

The next two days without Svadilfari, little work was done on the gate and, as darkness fell on the last night of winter, the builder knew that he could not keep his part of the bargain.

"I have been tricked!" exclaimed the builder angrily as he marched off to see the gods.

The gods laughed at the builder as he threatened and raged. Finally, they ordered him to leave. The builder refused unless he received his wages. Suddenly, Thor lifted his hammer and struck the builder a severe blow on the head. Loki's plan had worked!

Several months later, the white mare had a foal. But this was no ordinary foal. For one thing, the grey foal's father was Svadilfari, and for another, it had eight legs! Loki gave the foal to Odin. It was called Sleipnir and it became the finest horse in the world.

Idun and the Apples of Youth

One day long ago, Loki set out on a long journey with the gods Odin and Hoenir. They travelled over moorland and mountain until they reached a lonely valley. There they saw a herd of oxen grazing near a sparkling stream. The travellers were tired and

hungry so they sat down to rest. A short time later, they killed one of the oxen and lit a fire. They placed the animal on a spit over the flames and waited patiently for it to cook. The fire crackled, the flames rose but the meat remained raw. Loki decided to heap more wood on the fire and though the flames became hotter and hotter, still the ox would not cook.

As the travellers discussed why the meat stayed raw, they looked up and saw a large golden eagle perched on a branch of a nearby tree.

"I am preventing the meat from roasting," said the eagle. "I am hungry too. If you agree to give me share, the meat will be cooked in a very short time."

Reluctantly, the travellers agreed.

The meat began to sizzle and soon it was cooked. At once the eagle swooped down from the tree and greedily snatched nearly all of the meat. Loki was furious at this. He picked up a large stick and struck at the eagle with all his might. But the stick lodged in the eagle's body and, with Loki's hands still clinging to the stick, the eagle spread out its wings and flew high into the air.

"Help! Help!" shouted Loki, as the eagle soared higher above the lofty trees and over the craggy, snow-capped peaks. Loki now realised that this was no ordinary eagle - it was the giant Thiazi in disguise.

"I will help you," replied the eagle, "but on one condition only. You must promise to bring me the goddess Idun and her apples."

"I promise," said Loki.

At these words, the eagle released Loki, and the travellers completed their journey.

Now, Idun owned a casket in which she kept some magic apples. These apples were very special, for anyone who ate them - no matter how old - remained young and strong and brave. They were called the Apples of Youth and were eaten by the gods.

After several days, Loki went to visit Idun in Asgard, the kingdom of the gods.

"Idun," said Loki, "outside the walls of Asgard, I have discovered an apple tree. The apples on that tree appear fairer and sweeter than yours."

"That cannot be true," replied Idun, "for my apples are the fairest and sweetest in the whole world."

"Come with me and I'll show you," urged Loki, "but bring your casket of apples with you so that you can compare them with the others."

Never before had Idun taken the precious casket of apples outside the walls of Asgard, but she was so concerned at Loki's words that she agreed.

Loki and Idun started on their journey. They walked a long way until they reached a dark, lonely wood outside the kingdom of Asgard. They had not ventured very far into the wood when they stopped to rest. Perched high on one of the trees above them sat the eagle. As soon as Loki and Idun stopped, the eagle swooped down. Quickly it seized Idun and the casket of apples and carried them away to Thrymheim, its home.

A few days later, the gods who lived in Asgard, now growing old for want of the apples, wondered what had happened to Idun. They met together hoping to find some clue that might lead to her recovery. During the meeting one of the gods told how he had seen Idun leaving Asgard with Loki. At once Loki was summoned before the gods.

"Where is Idun and her apples, Loki?" they inquired.

"She is in Thrymheim with the giant Thiazi," replied Loki, "and the apples are with her."

"You must go to Thrymheim and bring back Idun and the apples," ordered the gods, "otherwise you will be punished most severely."

Loki was afraid of what the gods might do to him, so he agreed to travel to Thrymheim to try to find Idun. For the journey, the gods lent Loki the plumage of a hawk and off he flew to the land of the giants.

When Loki reached Thrymheim, he found that Thiazi the giant was not at home - he had gone fishing - and Idun was there alone. At once Loki used his magic power. He changed Idun into a nut. Still in the form of a hawk, with the nut clutched tightly in his claws, Loki flew high into the air to return to Asgard.

When the giant Thiazi arrived home and discovered that Idun had gone, he immediately changed himself into an eagle and soared away to Asgard.

Anxiously, the gods in Asgard waited for Loki's return. Soon they noticed a hawk approaching the walls of the kingdom. The bird was tightly clutching a nut and was followed closely by the eagle. The gods were afraid that Idun would be harmed, for the eagle flew even nearer to the hawk as it approached Asgard. The gods piled up a great heap of wood-shavings outside the wall. When the hawk dropped to the ground and was safely in Asgard the gods set fire to the shavings. The flames leapt high in the air and burned the eagle's feathers as it swooped down to land. The gods seized the eagle and killed it at once.

Loki now stood in his own form inside the walls of Asgard. After some magic words were spoken over the nut in Loki's hand, Idun and her casket of apples were restored. Idun gave one of her apples to each of the gods and they all became young and strong and brave again.

STORIES
FROM
FRANCE

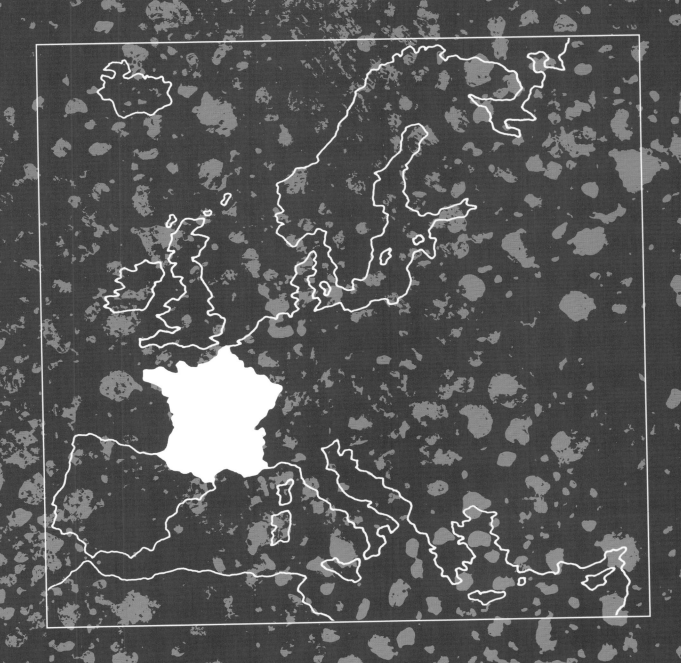

Reynard the Fox

Long ago, the lion was king of the animals in the forest. Every year, on the first day of spring, he held a banquet at his palace. All the animals were invited and they were delighted to attend - all except Reynard the fox. He had tricked and hurt so many of the other animals that he thought it wise to stay away from the feast.

Before the meal, the animals assembled in front of the lion and complained about Reynard's behaviour. When he had heard all the complaints, the lion was determined to bring the fox before him to answer for what he had done.

The lion summoned his advisers to discuss how best to capture the cunning fox and bring him to the palace. After much discussion it was agreed to send Tibert the cat, for he was wise and cunning too.

The cat was not very willing to go, but since the lion and his advisers had chosen him, he had no alternative but to agree. Tibert prepared for the journey and set off in search of the fox.

"I hope everything will go well," he whispered to himself. "I am really quite scared."

As he walked stealthily through the forest he saw a crow hovering above him. Tibert was superstitious and he thought that if the bird flew on his right side it would bring him good luck. Unfortunately, it flew past on his left side and this made him very worried. Nevertheless, Tibert continued his journey and after several hours reached Reynard's castle.

"Good evening, Reynard," said Tibert. "The lion has sent me to bid you attend his court. He wishes you to come immediately."

"Good evening, Tibert," replied Reynard. "How delightful to see you! I shall certainly accompany you to the lion's palace, but it is rather late now. I think we should wait until tomorrow morning."

Tibert was tired after his long walk and he agreed to wait.

"Tonight you will be my guest, Tibert," said Reynard. "What would you like to eat?"

"My favourite food is chicken," replied the cat, "but if you haven't a chicken some mice would be very tasty."

"I'm afraid I haven't a chicken, but not very far from here there is a barn where dozens of mice scurry from morning till night. Shall we go and catch some?" asked Reynard.

"Yes, I'd like that very much," answered Tibert, now feeling very hungry.

The fox and the cat set off through the dark forest until they reached the barn. Reynard knew this barn well, for the previous night he had burrowed a hole through the wall and had stolen one of the farmer's finest chickens. He also knew that the farmer had set a trap so that the next time he squeezed through the hole to steal a chicken he would be caught.

Reynard and Tibert waited patiently at the hole in the wall.

"Can you hear the mice scurrying across the floor?" asked Reynard. "There are dozens of them just waiting to be enjoyed. I'll stay here while you go and eat your fill."

Timidly, Tibert poked his head through the hole in the barn wall. Immediately, his neck was caught in the trap! The more he tugged and tried to wriggle free, the tighter the rope closed.

"How do the mice taste?" called Reynard. "I'm sure they are delicious."

Then Reynard slipped away leaving the cat crying and screaming for help.

The cat's cries and screams awakened the farmer and his family.

"Now we've caught the thief!" they shouted as they rushed out of the house and across the farmyard to the barn.

Luckily, Tibert managed to escape from them. Wearily, he crawled back to the lion's palace. The cunning Reynard had escaped again!

The Peasant and the Wolf

Long ago in France there lived a peasant called Pierre. One day, Pierre went to the market in a nearby village to buy bread. As he returned home through the forest, carrying two loaves of fresh bread, a lean, grey wolf appeared in front of him and growled fiercely. The peasant was terrified when he saw the wolf's gaping jaws and sharp teeth. Pierre realised that if he started to run away the wolf would surely catch him, so he stood still for a moment and thought about what he might do. Soon he had an idea.

"Good morning, Wolf," said Pierre, "you look hungry. Here is some bread for you."

He broke off a piece of bread from one of the loaves and threw it to the wolf. While the wolf was eating it, Pierre slipped away quietly. He had not gone very far when he heard a noise behind him. He turned round and there, a short distance away, was the wolf growling and snarling. Once more Pierre broke off a large chunk of bread and threw it to the wolf, hoping this would satisfy his hunger.

But no sooner had Pierre taken a few more steps through the forest than the wolf appeared behind him. Pierre broke off another piece of bread and threw it to the wolf. Then he went on his way again. This continued until the peasant, now exhausted, reached the cottage where he lived. His wife was waiting for him and when he appeared breathless at the door she wondered what was wrong.

"What is the matter my dear?" she inquired. "Have you seen a ghost in the forest? Where is the bread for supper?"

Pierre was so much out of breath that he could not answer her and he pointed towards the edge of the wood. There, his wife saw the snarling wolf approaching their cottage.

"A wolf!" she cried. "That's why you're out of breath. You're lucky it didn't devour you!"

Pierre had only one piece of bread left and before he went indoors he threw it to the wolf.

"There," he said, "you might as well have the last bit."

With a satisfied look, the wolf ate the bread and returned to the forest.

Some months later, Pierre and his wife had worked so hard that they had saved enough money to buy a cow.

One sunny morning, Pierre set off for the market in a nearby town where he hoped to find a cow cheap enough to buy. As he walked through the market looking at the cattle, a tall, thin stranger approached.

"Do you wish to buy a cow?" the stranger asked.

"Yes, I do," replied Pierre, "but I have very little money to spend. I am looking for a bargain."

"Then look no further," said the man. "I have some cows in my byre. I'm sure you will find a suitable one there. Follow me."

The two men walked briskly through the town until they reached a fine house. Behind the house stood a large byre. Pierre and the stranger stepped inside.

"Now," said the stranger, "choose any one you want and don't worry about the cost. I will give you the cow as a gift."

Pierre was amazed at the stranger's generosity, and he chose the one he wanted.

"You have made a wise choice," said the stranger. "I hope that she will give you plenty of milk for many years."

"Thank you very much, Sir," said Pierre, "but may I ask why you have been so kind to me?"

The stranger smiled.

"Do you remember several months ago you were kind to a wolf in the forest?" he asked. "You fed him with bread which was for you and your wife. Well, I was that wolf and I always return a kindness shown to me. Good luck and goodbye!"

STORIES
FROM
ENGLAND

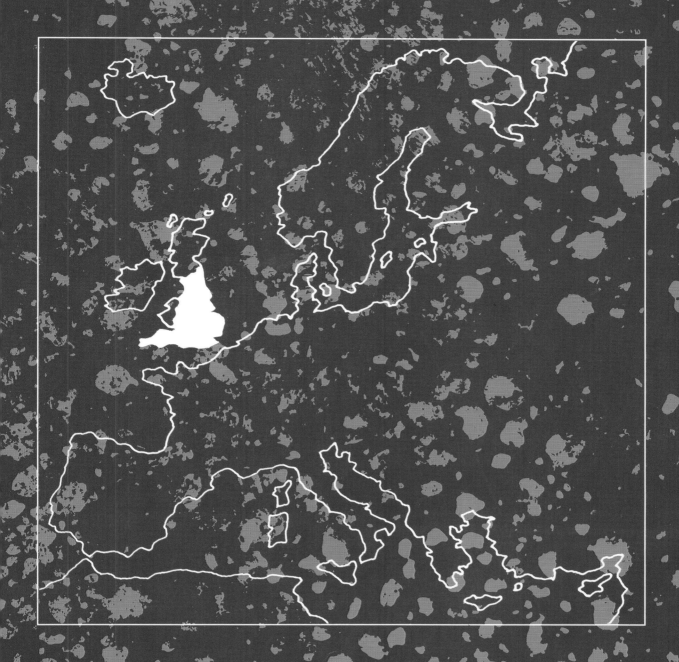

The Sword in the Stone

Long ago in England, there lived a king called Uther Pendragon. He and his wife had two children - a daughter Morgaus, and a son called Arthur. King Uther was strong and brave and he fought courageously against the Saxons who were attacking his country.

After several fierce attacks the king and his wife began to fear for the safety of their children. So Morgaus and Arthur were sent away to be looked after in the countryside where they would be much safer. Morgaus went to live at an abbey where she learned to read and write and cook and sew. Arthur's new home was with Sir Ector of Gwent. There he learned to ride and hunt and was brought up as a member of the knight's own family.

For a few years the king was successful in his struggle against his enemies. However, one winter's night he caught a fever and was no longer able to command his army. In a single battle many of his soldiers were killed. Soon the enemy marched towards St. Albans where they prepared for another attack.

Without their leader the English soldiers had no heart in fighting. So, on his sick-bed Uther was carried to the battlefield where he watched his soldiers fight more bravely than ever. But the noise and heat and excitement were too much for the king and that night he died peacefully on the journey home from the battlefield.

Not long after Uther Pendragon was buried, the noblemen of England began to dispute about who would be the next king. They argued and quarrelled but no agreement was reached. Then Merlin, the magician, had an idea and went to tell the bishop.

"My Lord Bishop," said Merlin, "I have an idea to settle the dispute about who will be the new king."

"You have?" inquired the bishop. "Tell me at once good man!"

"Summon all the noblemen in the country to London this Christmastide," replied Merlin. "Tell them that just as there was a miracle many years ago at this season, by another miracle, the new king will be revealed."

The bishop and the noblemen all laughed at Merlin's prophecy. Nevertheless, they decided to travel to London just to see if anything would happen.

On Christmas Eve, after the midnight service in the church, the bells pealed to announce that it was Christmas Day. The people rushed outside. There, on the green in front of the church, they noticed a huge stone. The stone was smooth and flat, and embedded in it was a gleaming sword. As the lights of the torches flamed in the frosty midnight air the bishop, the noblemen and the townsfolk could read the shimmering words on the glistening blade -

THIS SWORD IS EXCALIBUR. WHOEVER PULLS ME FROM THE STONE WILL BE THE RIGHTFUL KING.

The noblemen laughed when they saw the sword.

"Is this Merlin's miracle?" they jeered.

In spite of their jeers, one by one the noblemen approached the stone and tried to pull out the sword. Some pushed the sword from side to side, others banged it with logs of.wood. Many tugged and pulled it with all their might, but no one was able to loosen it even the slightest bit.

Then the bishop ordered that the sword and the stone should be covered by a tent and guarded by soldiers. Anyone who wished could still try to pull out the sword, but if by New Year's Day no one had succeeded, a tournament would be held and the winner would be crowned king.

In the days that passed between Christmas and New Year, men, both old and young, came to the church green and tried to loosen the sword. By the end of a week no one had been successful, so the tournament to decide who would be the new king would soon take place.

Early on New Year's Day, knights arrived from far and wide to prepare for the tournament. Among these were Sir Ector of Gwent, his son Kay and Arthur, Uther Pendragon's son, who, as a child had been sent to live at Ector's house in the country. Sir Ector was too old to take part in the tournament and Arthur was thought to be too young, so Kay was chosen to fight for the family.

On the morning of the contest, while Kay was swinging his sword above his head in practice for the fight, suddenly the sword struck

the sturdy trunk of an oak tree and the blade splintered into tiny pieces.

"My precious sword! My precious sword!" cried Kay. "I have broken my precious sword and it is too late to find another in time for the contest."

"Don't worry!" exclaimed Arthur. "I'll find another for you."

Immediately, Arthur set off to look for a sword. He searched everywhere in London, but all the blacksmiths were too busy to make a new sword for the tournament. No one would even lend Arthur a sword. Feeling tired and disappointed, Arthur trudged wearily back to tell Kay the sad news. Then, as he approached the church, he had an idea.

"The sword in the stone," he whispered. Arthur marched boldly towards the tent which housed the precious sword. The soldiers guarding it laughed and jeered.

"Well, young fellow, are you going to try your luck?" taunted one soldier.

"I'd like to, Sir. May I go in?" asked Arthur confidently.

The soldiers opened the flap and Arthur marched in. The young prince pulled with all his might. Immediately, the sword slid out of the stone, its sharp blade shimmering in the dim glow of the tent! While the soldiers ran to tell the bishop, Arthur was on his way to give the sword to Kay.

When he arrived at the house, Arthur waved the shining sword in the air.

"Look!" he shouted. "Here is Excalibur, the sword from the stone!"

Kay and Sir Ector were amazed.

"How did you get that precious sword?" demanded Sir Ector.

"I entered the tent, pulled the sword with all my might and out it came," replied Arthur.

Sir Ector was still rather doubtful about this explanation, so he took Arthur and Kay to the green where the tent was pitched. There, Arthur thrust the sword into the stone and pulled it out. He did this many times until Sir Ector and Kay were finally convinced.

Then Sir Ector told the people how Arthur was really the child of Uther Pendragon who had sent his son to him for protection during the war.

When Sir Ector had finished his story the bishop, the noblemen and the people knelt before Arthur to show that they accepted him as their new king. Merlin's miracle had happened!

Robin Hood meets Little John

Long ago in England, deep in the heart of Sherwood Forest, there lived a group of men who wished to help the poor. Robin Hood was their leader. He was strong and brave and was a fine shot with a bow and arrow.

One cold winter's day, Robin went to hunt deer in the forest. He walked along the bank of a swelling stream until he came to a tree which made a bridge over the fast-flowing waters. Suddenly, Robin heard some movement on the opposite bank. He paused for a moment. There, through the trees, he caught sight of a deer hiding in the undergrowth. Scarcely had he started to walk along the tree trunk, when he noticed a huge figure of a man about to cross from the other side. The man proceeded towards Robin and soon they met in the middle. The two stared at each other for a few seconds.

"Get out of my way!" shouted the big man, waving a large stick.

"I started out first," protested Robin, taking an arrow from his quiver and placing it on the string of the bow.

"You wouldn't be so bold without that bow and arrow!" replied the other.

"Oh yes I would!" exclaimed Robin Hood. "Wait here while I go and find a stick. We'll soon see."

Robin ran back to his side of the stream. With a sharp knife he cut a strong branch from a nearby tree and hurried across the stream to where his opponent was standing waiting. Immediately the two came face to face. Robin hit his opponent on the shoulder with the stick. The big man screamed with pain. Then he wielded his stick and hit Robin on the head. Robin was stunned. Nevertheless, using all his strength, he poked his opponent in the ribs with the stick. Again the man screamed. Suddenly, he pushed Robin so hard that he toppled him off the tree trunk into the cold waters of the stream.

"Now," said the man confidently, "I have won. I shall cross the stream first," and off he marched.

Out of the icy waters Robin scrambled and sat down on the bank beside his opponent.

"It was a fair fight," said Robin, "and you won. May I ask why you are in the forest?"

"I am looking for a group of men who live here. They have left their homes to help the poor. They are known as the Merry Men of Sherwood. Their leader is called Robin Hood. I would like to join this group. Do you know where I can find them?"

"I do," replied Robin. "I am Robin Hood."

The big man looked stunned.

"My men are camping not very far away," continued Robin. "Who are you?"

41

'MAJOR OAK' - ROBIN HOOD'S HIDING PLACE IN SHERWOOD FOREST
(Courtesy of **Nottinghamshire County Council**)

"My name is John Little," said the man.

"You will be made very welcome at my camp," said Robin. "I think we shall call you Little John!"

Off they went deeper into the forest where Little John met Friar Tuck, Alan-a-Dale and the other members of Robin's band.